Edouard Laboulaye

Finette

A Legend of Brittany

Edouard Laboulaye

Finette
A Legend of Brittany

ISBN/EAN: 9783337151645

Printed in Europe, USA, Canada, Australia, Japan

Cover: Foto ©Andreas Hilbeck / pixelio.de

More available books at **www.hansebooks.com**

FINETTE:

A

LEGEND OF BRITTANY.

TRANSLATED FROM THE FRENCH.

BOSTON:

J. E. TILTON AND COMPANY.

1867.

STEREOTYPED BY C. J. PETERS & SON,
13 Washington St., Boston.

————— ——

GEO. C. RAND & AVERY, Cornhill Press.

FINETTE.

FINETTE.

A LEGEND OF BRITTANY.

I.

ONCE upon a time there lived in Brittany a noble lord, called the Baron of Kerver. His manor was the finest in the province; the old Gothic chateau was all pointed arches,

and the walls were open-work like guipure lace.
On the first story, the picture-painted windows
opened on a balcony; six of them faced the east,
and six the west. In the morning, when the
baron, on his mare Isabel, went off to the forest,
followed by his blood-hounds, he saluted at each
window one of his daughters, who, prayer-book in
hand, prayed to Heaven for the house of Kerver.
To see their fair hair, blue eyes, and clasped
hands, you would have thought them six Madon-
nas in their azure niches.

When, at setting sun, the baron returned home,
after having traversed his domains, he saw from
afar, in the western windows, six sons, with brown
hair, and bold air, the hope and glory of the
family. They looked like six chevaliers, sculp-
tured on the doorway of a church. So, for ten
leagues round, when they wished to name a happy
father and a powerful baron, it was always the
Baron Kerver. The chateau had only twelve
windows, and the baron had thirteen children.

The last one, who had no place, was a handsome boy of sixteen, called Yvon. As usual, he was the favorite. When the baron went off in the morning, and when he returned at night, Yvon was always waiting on the doorstep to embrace him. With his fair hair which reached to his waist, his lithe figure, defiant air, and bold carriage, Yvon was the idol of all the people. When twelve years old, he had already bravely attacked and killed a wolf with his hatchet; from which he received the nickname of *Sans-Peur*, a title that he well merited, for there never was a braver heart.

One day, when the baron remained at home, and for amusement was breaking a lance with his squire, Yvon, in travelling dress, entered the hall, and, bending one knee, "My lord and father," said he to the

baron, "I come to ask your blessing, and to say
farewell. The house of Kerver is rich in chevaliers, and does not need a child: it is time for me
to seek my fortune. I wish to go away, try my
strength, and make a·name for myself."

"You are right, Sans-Peur," replied the baron,
more moved than he cared to show; "I will not
keep you; I have no right to keep you: but you
are very young; perhaps it would be better for
you to stay another year with us."

" I am sixteen years old, father. At my age
you had already fought against a Rohan. I have
not forgotten that our arms are a unicorn destroying a lion, and our motto, '*Forward.*' I
do not want the Kervers to blush for their last
child."

Yvon received his father's blessing, shook
hands with his brothers, kissed his sisters, bade
good-by to all the vassals, who wept, and departed with a light heart.

Nothing stopped him on his journey. He
swam the rivers, climbed the mountains, and
traversed the woods by following the sun. " Forward, Kervers!" he cried when he encountered
any obstacle, and willy nilly he always marched
straight forward.

He had wandered three years through the
world, seeking adventures, sometimes victorious,
sometimes defeated, but always merry and bold,
when he was asked to join a crusade against the
Norwegian heathen. To kill miscreants and

gain a kingdom was a double pleasure. Yvon found twelve brave comrades, chartered a little ship, and unfurled from the masthead a blue banner, with the unicorn and motto of the Kerver.

The sea was calm, the wind favorable, the night clear. Yvon, lying on deck, watched the stars, and looked for that one that shone over his paternal home, when suddenly the ship struck a rock,

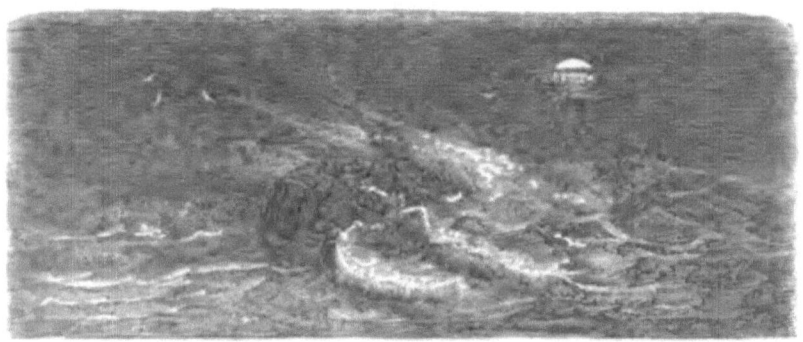

a horrible cracking was heard, the masts fell like dead wood, and a huge wave broke over the deck, sweeping off all on it.

" Forward, Kervers!" cried Yvon as he rose

to the surface; and he began to swim as quietly as if he were bathing in the castle pond. Happily, the moon soon rose, and Yvon perceived afar off a black spot in the midst of the silvered waves: that was land. He approached it with difficulty, and at length landed. Being wet to the skin, exhausted, and out of breath, he flung himself on the sand, and, without worrying, said his prayers, and slept.

II.

ON awaking in the morning, Yvon tried to recognize the country where chance had thrown him. He perceived afar off a house as large as a cathedral, with windows fifty feet high. He walked a whole day before reaching it, and at length saw before him an immense door, with a knocker so heavy that no man's hand could lift it. Yvon took a huge stone, and knocked.

"Come in!" said a voice which resounded like the bellow of a bull. At the same instant the door opened, and the little Breton found himself face to face with a giant, who was at least forty feet high.

"What is your name? and what are you doing here?" said the giant, seizing our adventurer by the collar, and lifting him up in order to see him more easily.

"I am called Sans-Peur, and I am seeking my

fortune," replied Yvon, regarding the monster
with an air of defiance.

"Well, brave Sans-Peur, your fortune is made,"
said the giant mockingly: "I am in need of a
servant, and I will take you. You can begin
your duties now. This is the time that I take

my flock to pasture; and you must clean the
stable. I will not give you any thing more to
do," he added, grinning: "you see that I am a
good master. Do your work; and, above all,
don't wander about the house, or your life will
be the forfeit."

"Truly I have a good master: my work is not
hard," said Yvon when the giant had gone. "I
have time enough to sweep the stable: what shall
I do meanwhile to amuse myself? Suppose I
look round the house? As I have been for-
bidden to do so, there must be something to
see."

He entered the first room. There was a large
fireplace, with a pot hanging on the chimney-
hook. The pot was boiling, though there was
no fire on the hearth.

"How is that?" said Yvon: "there is some
mystery there!" He cut off a lock of his hair,
dipped it in the pot, and drew it out covered
with copper.

"Oh! oh!" cried he; "here is a new kind of soup: by swallowing it we might have a cuirass in the stomach."

He passed into the second room. There again he saw a pot hanging on the chimney-hook, boiling without fire. Yvon dipped in it a lock of hair, and drew it out covered with silver.

"In the Kerver mansion," he thought, "the soup is not so rich, but perhaps it tastes better." Whereupon he entered the third room. There also was a pot hanging on the chimney-hook, boiling without fire. Yvon dipped in it a lock of hair, and drew it out covered with gold. It shone so that it looked like sunlight.

"Good!" cried he: "in Brittany we have a proverb that says, *Every thing goes from bad to worse;* here, on the contrary, every thing goes from good to better. What shall I find in the fourth chamber? — a diamond soup?"

He pushed open the door, and saw something more rare than precious stones, — a young lady

of such marvellous beauty, that Yvon, dazzled by
the sight of her, fell on his knees.

"Unhappy man!" she cried in a trembling
voice, "what do you here?"

"I am one of the household," replied the Breton; "the giant has taken me into his service."

"Into his service!" rejoined the young lady.
"May Heaven remove you from it!"

"Why so?" said Yvon. "I have a good master; the work is not hard. The stable once
swept, my task is done."

"Yes, and how will you set about it?" asked

the stranger. "If you do like every one else, for
every pitchfork of muck that you throw out of
the door, ten will come in the window. I will
tell you what you must do. Turn the pitchfork,
sweep with the handle; the muck will rush out
of itself at one stroke."

"I will obey," said Yvon; and then sat down
by the young lady, and began to talk to her. She
was the daughter of a fairy whom the wicked
giant had made his slave. Friendship soon
springs up between companions in misfortune:
before the end of the day, Finette (that was the
lady's name) and Yvon had already promised to
marry one another, if they could escape from
their horrid master. The difficulty was to find
a way.

Time flies fast in such conversation. Night
approached, and Finette sent away her new
friend, advising him to sweep the stable before
the giant returned.

Yvon took the pitchfork, and, without being

too wise, he thought to use it as he had seen it used in his father's castle; but he soon had enough of it, for in less than an instant the stable was so filled that the poor fellow had no place to stand in. He then did as Finette had told him, turned the fork, and swept with the handle. In the twinkling of an eye, the stable was as clean as if it had never been used.

His task ended, Yvon seated himself on a bench at the door of the house. As soon as he saw the giant coming, he tossed up his head, and drummed with his feet, while singing a song of his country.

"Have you cleaned the stable?" demanded the giant, frowning.

"All is ready, master," replied Yvon, without moving.

"I'll see about that," growled the giant. He strode, scolding, to the stable, found all in order, and came forth furious.

"You have seen my Finette," he cried; "the

trick did not come out of your brain."

"What is '*my finette*'?" said Yvon, opening his mouth and shutting his eyes. "Is it a beast of this country, master? Let me see it."

"Hold your tongue, fool!" replied the giant; "you will see her only too soon."

The next day, the giant collected his sheep to take them to the fields; but, before starting, he ordered Yvon to go that morning and

bring his horse, which was at grass on the mountain. "After that," said he, grinning, "you can
rest the whole of the day. You see I am a good
master. Do your work; and, above all, don't
wander about the house, or I will cut off your
head."

Yvon let him pass, and winked his eye.

"Truly," said he between his teeth, "you are
a good master; malice does not choke you: but,
spite of your threats, I am going into the house
to talk to Finette. We will see if your Finette
does not belong to me instead of you."

He hurried to the young lady's room. "Vic-
tory!" cried he on entering: "I have nothing
to do all day but go to the mountain and bring
home his horse."

"Very well," said Finette, "how will you set
about it?"

"That is a fine question," returned Yvon. "Is
it a hard matter to ride a horse? I think I have
mounted worse ones than he."

"It is not as easy as you think," replied Finette; "but I will tell you how you must do.
When you approach the animal, fire and flame
will come out of his nostrils as if out of a fur-
nace: but take the bridle which is hidden behind
the stable-door, and throw it right between the
horse's teeth; he will then become as gentle as
a lamb, and you may do with him what you
please."

"I will obey," said Yvon; and then sat down
by Finette, and began to talk to her. What did

they talk of? Of every
thing, and more too; but,
however far their fancies
led them, they always re-
turned to the fact that
they would marry one
another, and that they must escape from the
giant. Time flies fast in such conversation.
Night approached: Yvon had forgotten the horse
and the mountain. Finette was obliged to send

him away, advising him to bring back the animal
before the master's return.

Yvon took the bridle that was hidden behind
the stable-door, and ran to the mountain.   There

he saw a horse almost as large as an elephant,
who came galloping toward him, snorting forth
fire and flame.

Yvon awaited firmly the enormous beast, and,

when he opened his jaws, flung in the bridle. Instantly the horse became as gentle as a lamb. Yvon made him kneel down, climbed on his back, and returned quietly home.

His task ended, our Breton seated himself on the bench at the door of the house. As soon as he saw the giant coming, he tossed up his head, and drummed with his feet, while singing a song of his country.

"Have you brought back my horse?" demanded the giant, frowning.

"Yes, master," replied Yvon, without moving. "That is a fine beast, and does you honor: he is gentle, pretty, and well taught. He is eating in the stable."

"I'll see about that," growled the giant. He entered scolding, found all in order, and came forth furious. "You have seen my Finette," he cried: "the trick did not come out of your brain."

"Master," said Yvon, opening his mouth and shutting his eyes, "you have always the same story. What is '*my finette*'? Once for all, let me see that monster."

"Hold your tongue, fool!" replied the giant. "You will see her only too soon."

The next day, at dawn, the giant collected his sheep to take them to the fields; but, before going, he said to Yvon, "To-day you must go into the bowels of the earth to collect my rent. After that," he continued, grinning, "you can rest the whole of the day. You see that I am a good master"

"A good master indeed," murmured Yvon; "but the task is none the less hard. I will go and see my Finette, as the giant says: I have great need of her aid to-day."

When Finette had asked her friend what was his task for the day, " Well," said she, " how will you set about it this time? "

" I do not know," answered Yvon, sadly. " I have never been into the bowels of the earth; and, even if I knew the way there, I should not know what to ask for. Tell me: I will obey."

" Do you see that huge rock down there? " said Finette: " that is one of the doors of hell. Take this stick; strike the rock with it three times, and a demon will come forth wrapped in flames. You must tell him the object of your visit, and he will ask you how much you want. Be careful to answer, ' Not more than I can carry.' "

" I will obey," said Yvon; and then sat down by Finette, and began to talk to her. He would be there now, if, at the approach of night, the young lady had not sent him to the huge rock to execute the task the giant had set him.

When he reached the place, Yvon found a large block of granite: that he struck three times with the stick; the rock opened, and a demon came out, wrapped in flames.

"What do you want?" he cried in a terrible voice.

"I have come to collect the giant's rent," replied Yvon, composedly.

"How much do you want?"

"Not more than I can carry," replied the Breton.

"It is well for you that you do not ask for

more," returned the flaming demon. "Enter this cavern: you will find what you seek."

Yvon entered, and stared with astonishment. All about lay gold, silver, diamonds, carbuncles, and emeralds, strewn as thick as the sands of the sea.

He filled a sack, threw it on his shoulder, and returned home.

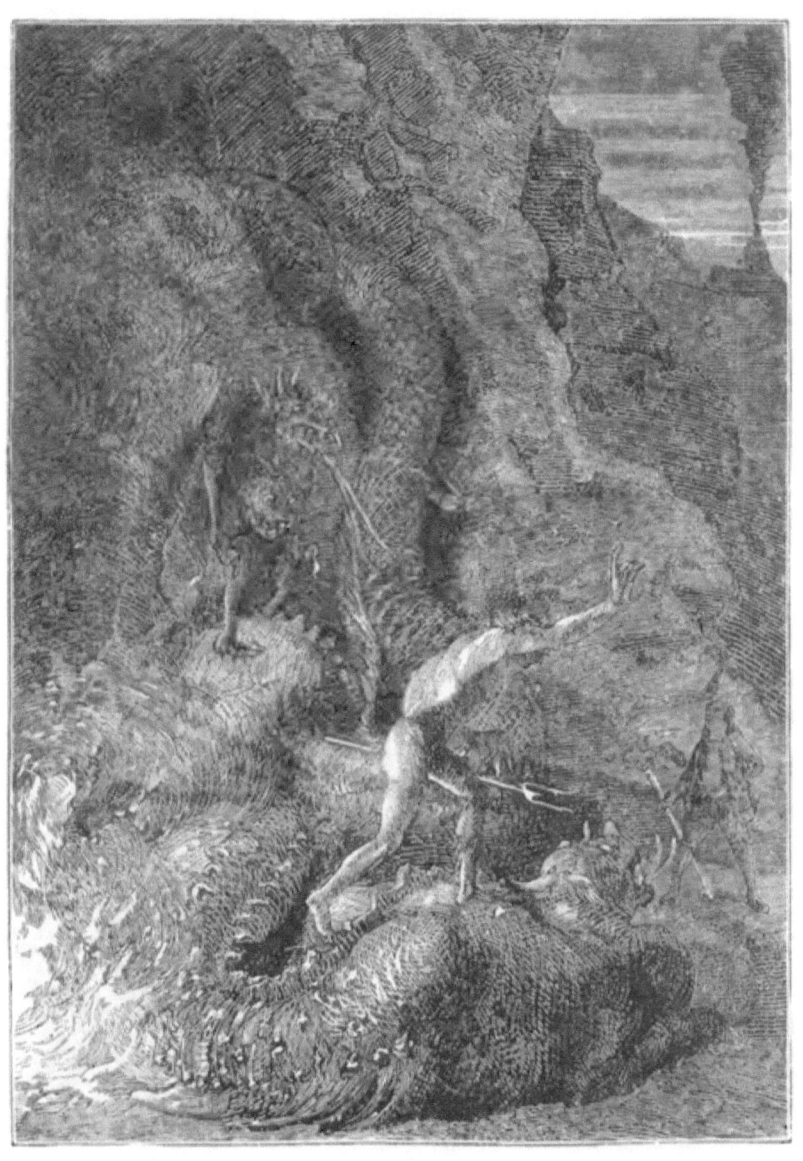

"What do you want?" he cried in a terrible voice.

His task ended, our Breton seated himself on the bench at the door of the house. As soon as he saw the giant coming, he tossed up his head, and drummed with his feet, while singing a song of his country.

"Have you been down to collect my rent?" demanded the giant, frowning.

"Yes, master," replied Yvon, without moving. "That sack there will dazzle your eyes. The amount is inside."

"I'll see about that," growled the giant. He untied the strings of the bag, which was so full that gold and silver rolled out in every direction. "You have seen my Finette," he cried: "the trick did not come out of your brain."

"Master," said Yvon, opening his mouth and shutting his eyes, "you only know one song: it is always the same refrain, — '*My finette, my finette!*' Once for all, show me that thing."

"Very well," said the giant, howling with fury; "wait till to-morrow, I will let you make her acquaintance."

"Many thanks, master," said Yvon: "you are very kind; but, from your merry face, I am sure you are jesting with me."

III.

THE next day, the giant departed without giving any order to Yvon, which worried Finette. At noon he returned without his sheep, complaining of fatigue and the heat, and said to the young lady:

"You will find at the door my servant. Cut off his head; put it to boil in the big pot; and, when the soup is ready, call me."

Then he stretched himself on the bed, and went to sleep, and snored so loud that it sounded like thunder.

Finette made all ready, took a large knife, and called Yvon. She then pricked his little finger,

and three drops of blood fell on the chopping-
block.

"That will do," said the young lady: "now
help me to fill the pot."

They threw into it every thing they could
find, — old coats, old shoes, old carpets, and the
rest! Then Finette took Yvon by the hand, led
him into the three entrance-chambers, cast in a
mould three golden balls, two silver ones, and
one of copper, and, running out of the house,
took the road to the sea.

"Forward, Kervers!" cried Yvon when he found himself out of doors. "Tell me, dear Finette, what farce we are playing now."

"Let us save ourselves," said she. "If, by setting sun, we have not escaped from this dreadful island, all is over with us."

"Forward, Kervers!" cried Yvon, laughing; "and a fig for the giant."

After the giant had snored an hour, he stretched his legs, opened the corner of one eye, and cried:

"Is it almost ready?"

"It has begun," replied the first drop of blood on the chopping-block.

The giant turned over, and snored for another hour or two. Then he stretched his legs, opened the corner of one eye, and cried:

"Do you hear me? Is it almost ready?"

"It simmers," replied the second drop of blood on the chopping-block.

The giant turned over, and slept another hour.

Then he stretched out his long limbs, and cried impatiently:

" Is not all ready?"

" All is ready," replied the third drop of blood upon the chopping-block.

The giant sat up in bed, rubbed his eyes,

and looked to see who had spoken, but saw no one.

"Finette!" he howled, "why is not the table laid?"

No answer. The giant, furious, leaped from the bed, took his spoon, which looked like a kettle stuck on a pitch-fork, and plunged it into the pot to taste the soup.

"Finette!" he howled, "you have not salted it! What sort of soup is this? I find neither fat nor lean in it!"

No; but, in return, he found his carpet, which was not quite boiled away. At the sight of it, he became so enraged that his knees shook under him.

"Wretches!" he cried, "you have fooled me; but you shall pay for it."

He rushed out with his stick in his hand, and took such long strides, that at the end of a quarter of an hour he discovered the fugitives still far from the river: then he uttered a cry of joy which made the echoes ring for twenty leagues around.

Finette stopped, all trembling: Yvon clasped her close to him."

"Forward, Kervers!" he exclaimed: "the sea is not far distant; we shall reach it before our enemy."

"Oh! see him! see him!" cried Finette, pointing to the giant, who was not more than a hundred paces off. "We are lost, unless this talisman saves us."

She took the ball of copper, and threw it on the ground, crying: ·

> "Ball of copper, he is nigh;
> Save us quickly, ere we die."

Instantly the ground yawned asunder with a frightful noise. An enormous gulf, a bottomless abyss, arrested the giant as he stretched out his hand to seize his prey.

"Let us fly!" cried Finette, seizing Yvon by
the arm, as he stood watching the giant, and
singing at the top of his lungs:

> "Old bugbear! old bugbear!
> You have fallen in a snare!"

The giant began to rage up and down before the
gulf like a caged bear, trying to cross, and finding no way. At length, with a furious pull, he
uprooted an immense oak, and threw it across,
the branches nearly destroying the poor children
in its fall. The giant then straddled across this
bridge that shook beneath him; and thus sus-
pended beneath heaven and earth, he slowly
advanced, constantly obliged to disentangle himself from the branches. When he reached the
other side, Yvon and Finette were already on
the shore, the sea rolling at their feet. Alas!
there was neither boat nor ship: the fugitives
were lost. Yvon, always brave, picked up peb-

"Let us fly!" cried Finette, seizing Yvon by the arm, as he
stood watching the giant, and singing at the top of his lungs.

bles to throw at the giant, that he might sell his life as dearly as possible. Finette, trembling, took one of the silver balls, and flung it into the sea, crying:

> "Ball of silver, precious friend,
> Quickly succor to us send."

Hardly had she pronounced the magic words before a fine ship lay upon the water, looking like a swan spreading its white wings to the breeze. Yvon and Finette rushed into the water; a rope was flung to them; and, by the time the furious giant reached the shore, the ship was under full sail, leaving a long track of shining foam behind.

Giants do not like water; that is declared to be true by old Homer, who knew Polyphemus: the same thing is mentioned in all Natural Histories worthy of the name. Finette's master was like Polyphemus: he roared aloud on seeing his slaves escape him, ran up and down the shore,

hurled enormous rocks after the ship, which luckily did not touch it, and only made black holes in the sea; then, beside himself with rage, he plunged into the water, and began to swim with incredi‑ble speed after the ship. At every stroke, he advanced forty feet, snorting like a whale. Little by little, he gained on his enemies, and needed but one more stroke to reach the gunwale; already his arm was stretched out to seize it, when Finette threw the second

silver ball into the sea, and cried aloud, weeping :

"Ball of silver, precious friend,
Quickly succor to us send."

Suddenly, from the midst of the spouting foam,
there issued a gigantic swordfish. He rushed

upon the giant, who had only time to dive;
chased him under the water, on top of the waves,
pursued him through all his doublings, and forced

him with great speed home to his island, which
he reached at last with great difficulty, and fell
upon the sand, dripping, furious, and beaten.

"Forward, Kervers!" cried Yvon; "we are
saved."

"Not yet," replied Finette, trembling. "The
giant has a godmother who is a sorceress: I fear
she will revenge on me the injury done to her
godson. My art tells me that if you leave me
for only a single instant, my dear Yvon, I have
every thing to fear, until the day when you be-
stow upon me your name in the chapel of Kerver Castle."

"By the unicorn of my ancestors!" said Yvon,
"you have the soul of a hare, my dear Finette,
and not of a Breton woman. Am I not with
you? Do I mean to leave you? Do you think
that Heaven has saved us from the clutches of
that horrible giant to drown us in port?"

He smiled so sweetly, and showed such beautiful white teeth, that Finette smiled at her own

fears. Ah, youth! youth! your sorrows are so
fleeting! the sun shines so soon after a storm!
your sorrows are sweeter than our happiness!

IV.

THE rest of the voyage passed pleasantly
enough: it seemed as though an invisible hand
pushed the ship towards Brittany. Twenty days
after their departure, the ship's boat deposited
the two voyagers in a bay by the Castle of
Kerver.

Once landed, Yvon turned to thank his pre-
servers, but all had vanished; ship and all had
sunk beneath the waves, leaving no more trace
behind than the wing of a sea-gull.

Yvon recognized the spot where, as a child, he
had often picked up shells, and chased crabs
into their holes. Before half an hour, he would

see the arches and towers of the old manor-house.
His heart beat, and he glanced tenderly at Finette.　Then he saw, for the first time, that she

had on a singular dress, not suitable for a lady
who was about to enter the noble house of
Kerver.

"My dear child," said he, "my father, the
baron, is a noble lord, accustomed to great respect.　I cannot present you to him in that Bo-
hemian costume; and it is not fitting that you

should enter our castle on foot,—that will do
for the peasant folk. Wait for me a few mo-
ments, and I will bring you the garments and
palfrey of one of my sisters. I wish you to be
received like a lady of high degree, so that my
father himself shall descend the staircase on
your arrival, and request the honor of conduct-
ing you."

"Yvon, Yvon!" said Finette, "do not leave
 me, I beg of you. Once
back in your old home,
you will forget me, I know."

"Forget you!" cried
Yvon. "If any one but
you had so insulted me,
I would have taught him, sword in hand,
what it is to insult a Kerver. Forget you, Finette! You do not know the constancy of a
Breton."

The Bretons are constant, doubtless, but they
are very obstinate. Poor Finette in vain be-

sought in the tenderest manner: she was forced
to yield. At length, resigned against her will,
she said to Yvon:

"Go, then, to your castle, but do not stop to
greet any one: hasten to the stables, and return
as quickly as possible. They will all surround
you; pretend not to see them, and, above all, be
sure to eat and drink nothing. Should you take
even a glass of water, misfortune will happen to
us both."

Yvon swore to obey Finette, but in his heart
he laughed at her woman's weakness. He felt
sure of himself, and thought proudly that a
Breton was not like those giddy Frenchmen
whose faith is said to be broken at the slightest
touch.

When our adventurer entered the castle, he
could scarcely recognize it. The windows, both
outside and in, were festooned with flowers, and
the court-yard was strewn with fresh green. On
one side were huge tables, bountifully spread,

where cider flowed like water; on the other side, fiddlers, mounted on barrels, scraped merrily away. The vassals and their wives and daughters, all dressed in their best, danced and sung. It was a high holiday, in short: the baron himself smiled. That day he married his fifth daughter to the Chevalier de Kernavalee, and the noble union added another coat of arms to his shield.

Yvon, recognized and saluted by the crowd,

was soon surrounded by his family. They embraced him, and, holding his hands, asked where he had been, and whence he came. Had he conquered a kingdom, a duchy, or a baronetcy? Had he brought for the bride royal jewels? Had the fairies protected him? How many rivals had he overthrown in the tournament? All these questions mingled confusedly together. Yvon respectfully kissed his father's hand, ran to his sisters' chamber, took two of their prettiest dresses, went to the stable, saddled a palfrey, and, mounted on a beautiful Spanish jennet, was about to leave the castle, when he found before him his relations, friends, and vassals, who, glasses in hand, wished to drink to the happy return of their young lord.

Yvon thanked them gracefully, and waved his hand to the friendly crowd while slowly making his way on, when, at the entrance, by the sunken draw-bridge, a lady whom he did not know, the bridegroom's sister perhaps, a blonde, with a

haughty and disdainful air, approached him, holding an apple between two fingers.

"Noble sir," said she, with a strange smile,
"you will not refuse a lady's first request. Taste

the apple, I beg of you.
After so long a journey,
if you are neither hungry
nor thirsty, you have not, at
least, forgotten the laws of
gallantry.

Yvon could not resist
this appeal; and there he
did wrong, for scarcely had
he tasted the apple before
he looked around him like
one awaked from a dream.

"What am I doing on
this horse?" he thought. "What means this
palfrey that I am leading away? Is not my
place at home during my sister's wedding?
Why should I leave the castle?"

He threw the bridle of his horse to an attend-
ant, leaped lightly down, and offered his hand to
the fair lady, who instantly accepted him as her
escort, and, by special favor, gave him her
bouquet to hold.

Before the end of the evening, there were
two more betrothed within the castle. Yvon had
promised to marry the stranger. Finette was
forgotten.

V.

SEATED on the sea-shore, poor Finette waited all day for Yvon; but Yvon never came. The sun was setting behind the red waves, when Finette rose, sighing, and, in her turn, took the road to the castle. She had not walked long through a narrow lane bordered with heather in bloom, before she saw before her an old tumble-down hut, at the door of which a toothless old crone ·was preparing to milk her cow. Finette approached the dame, and, after dropping a low curtsey, asked her for a night's lodging.

The old woman looked at the stranger from head to foot. With her fur-topped boots, long, brown petticoat, blue jacket bordered with jet, and head-dress, Finette looked more like an Egyptian than a Christian. The old woman frowned, and, shaking her fist at the poor girl, —

"Begone, sorceress!" she cried: "there is no room for you in an honest dwelling."

"Good mother," said Finette, "give me, then, a corner in your barn."

"Yes," said the old woman, laughing, and show-ing her single tooth, which stuck straight out,

"you want a corner in my barn. You can have
it, wretch, when you have filled my milking-pail
with gold!"

"Agreed," said Finette, quietly.

She opened a leathern purse at her belt, drew
out a golden ball, and threw it in the pail, saying:

> "Ball of gold, oh, lend your aid
> To rescue an unhappy maid!"

And behold pieces of gold dancing in the bottom

of the pail. They rose higher
and higher, leaping up like
fish in a net, while the old
woman, on her knees, watched
every thing, dumb with won-
der. When the pail was full,
the old woman rose, took it
on her arm, and, curtseying to Finette,—

"Madam," cried she, "every thing belongs to
you,—house, the cow, and all. I am going to the

city, where I shall live like a lady, and do nothing.

Ah! if I only were not sixty years old!" And, hobbling on her crutch, she started off, without looking back, for the Kerver Castle.

Finette entered the hut: it was a horrible place, dark and damp, full of dirt and spiders' webs; a sad home for a woman accustomed to live in the giant's grand chateau. Finette quietly approached the hearth, where some bits of damp heather were smouldering; and, drawing out of her purse another golden ball, threw it on the fire, saying:

> "Ball of gold, oh, lend your aid
> To rescue an unhappy maid!"

Instantly gold burst forth, and spread all over the house like running water; every thing, the

whole house, the walls and roof, the wooden
benches, the stools, the bed, the cow's horns,
even the spiders and their webs, were changed
into gold. In the moonlight, the house sparkled
amid the trees like a star in a dark night.

When Finette had milked the cow, and drunk
a little of the milk, she threw herself, all dressed,
on the bed, and, tired out by the fatigues of the
day, cried herself to sleep.

Old women do not know how to hold their
tongues, at least in Brittany. As soon as Finette's hostess reached the little village lying at
the foot of the Kerver Castle she went straight
to the village squire. He was an important per-
sonage, who had often made the old woman

tremble when she inadvertently allowed her cow
to pasture in a neighbor's field. The squire
listened to her tale, and shook his head several
times, saying that there was a suspicion of heresy
about it. Then he brought, mysteriously, a pair
of scales, tried the pieces of gold that he found

unalloyed and of the true ring, pocketed as many of them as he could, and ended by advising her to tell no one of the strange adventure.

" If the bailiff or the seneschal hear of it," said he," the least that will happen will be the loss of your gold. Justice is impartial; without favor or reputation, it takes every thing."

The old woman thanked the squire for his advice, and determined to follow it. So, by night, she had only told her story to two neighbors,

her dearest friends, and both of them had sworn secrecy on their little children's heads, — a

solemn oath, so well kept that by noon the next
day there was not a child of six years old in
the village who did not point
at the old woman. Even the
dogs, when barking, seemed
to say, "Hold! hold! the old
woman with gold!"

Girls that fill pails with gold are not found
every day. Even were she a little bit of a
sorceress, such a girl would not be the less a
treasure in a house. The squire, who was un-

married, made this wise reflection on going to
bed, and arose at daybreak to visit the stranger.
By the faint morning light, he saw something
shining afar off in the woods, and was much
astonished when, instead of the miserable hut,

he found a golden house. But he was more
charmed and astonished when, on entering the

palace, he saw seated by the window a beautiful girl with black hair, who was plying her distaff with the majesty of a queen.

Like all men, the squire had a good opinion of himself, and felt, in the bottom of his heart, that there was not a woman in the world who would not be overjoyed to marry him. So, without hesitation, he declared to Finette that he had come to marry her. The young girl began to laugh, and the squire grew furious.

"Take care," said he in a terrible voice," I am master here. No one knows who you are, or whence you came. That gold you gave the old woman is suspicious : there is magic in this house. If you do not instantly accept me for your husband, I will arrest you; and, before evening perhaps, you will be burnt for a witch in front of the castle."

"You are very kind," said Finette, making up a charming face:" you have a peculiar way of your own of courting ladies. Even when they have decided, a gallant chevalier respects their scruples and their modesty."

"We Bretons," replied the squire, "are very free-spoken; we go right to the point. Marriage or prison! Choose."

"Good!" said Finette, laying down her distaff. "See, the fire has fallen into the room."

"Don't move," returned the squire: "I will put back the sticks on the hearth."

"Fix the fire well," said Finette: "poke out the ashes. Have you the tongs?"

"Yes," answered the squire, who at that moment was picking up the hot coals.

"*Abracadabra!*" cried Finette, rising. "May the tongs hold you, and you hold the tongs, until sunset!"

No sooner said than done. The wicked squire remained there all day,

knocking away with the tongs the live coals that
flew up in his face, and the ashes that came in
his eyes. In vain he cried, prayed, wept, and
cursed: no one heard him. If Finette had remained at home, she would, without doubt, have
taken pity on him; but, after having cursed him,
she ran down to the sea. There, unmindful of
every thing, she waited for Yvon, who never
came.

As soon as the sun had set, the tongs fell from
the squire's hands. He waited for nothing, but
began to run as if the devil, or justice herself,
were at his heels. He gave such leaps, and
groaned so loud, was so blackened, singed, and
paralyzed, that every one in the village was afraid
of him. The boldest tried to speak to him; but
he ran on without answering, and took refuge in
his house, more ashamed than a wolf who had
caught his paw in a trap.

In the evening, when poor Finette returned
home, she found, in place of the squire, a visitor

who was none the less formidable. The bailiff
had heard the story of the pieces of gold, and
had also determined to marry the stranger. He
was not so brutal as the squire, but was fat and
merry. He could not speak without laughing,

showing his large yellow teeth, and puffing like
an ox. In reality, he was not less persistent or
threatening than his predecessor. Finette be-
sought him to leave her alone; but the bailiff

burst out laughing, and kindly informed his darling, that, by virtue of his office, he could imprison and hang without process of law. Finette clasped her hands and wept. For answer, the baliff drew out of his pocket a roll of parchment, on which he had written a promise of marriage; and he declared, that, should he be obliged to pass the night in the house, he would not leave until it was signed.

" Besides," he added, "if my person does not please you, I will not insist. I have another piece of parchment here, on which I can write

something quite different; and, if the sight of me offends you, it is very easy to shut your eyes."

While speaking, he clasped his throat with his hand, and hung his tongue out in a very agreeable way, calculated to amuse.

"Alas!" said Finette, "I might perhaps make up my mind to do as you wish, if I were sure of finding in you a good husband; but I am afraid."

"Of what, my dear child?" said the smiling bailiff, already as proud as a peacock.

"Do you think," she answered with a saucy air, "that a good husband would leave that door open, and not remember that the wind was blowing on his wife?"

"You are right, my beauty," replied the bailiff. "I am a blundering fellow; but I will repair my fault."

"Have you hold of the handle?" demanded Finette.

"Yes, my pretty one," replied the happy bailiff. "I am going to shut it."

"*Abracadabra!*" cried Finette. "May the door hold you, wicked man, and you hold the door, until daybreak."

And the door began to open and shut, and

knock against the wall like an eagle beating its wings. Imagine the dance it led the poor cap-

tive during a long night. He had never danced such a waltz before, and, I imagine, never wished to dance a second. Sometimes he pushed the door into the street; sometimes the door pushed him against the wall, and nearly crushed him to death. He went to and fro, crying, swearing, weeping, and praying: all in vain, for the door was deaf, and Finette was asleep.

At daybreak his numbed fingers opened, and he fell into the road, head foremost. Without waiting for any thing, he began to run as if the Saracens were after him. He never even turned round, fearing that the door was at his heels. Luckily, every one was asleep when he reached the village óf Kerver, and he was able to hide his sad countenance in bed without being seen; a fortunate chance, for he was white from head to foot, and so haggard and trembling that he would have been taken for the ghost of a miller.

When Finette opened her eyes, she saw by her bed a large man dressed in black, with a velvet cap and a sword, like a chevalier. He was the seneschal of the court and baronetcy of Kerver. His arms were crossed, and he was looking at the young girl in a way that froze her blood with horror.

"What is your name, vassal?" said he in a voice of thunder.

"Finette, at your service, my lord," she replied, trembling.

"Does this house and furniture belong to you?"

"Yes, my lord," said she; "it is all at your service."

"That is the way I understand it," replied the gloomy seneschal. "Get up, vassal: I do you the honor of marrying you, and of taking you and your goods under my protection."

"My lord," said Finette, "you are too kind to a poor girl like me. I am only a stranger, without friends or relations."

"Hold your tongue, vassal!" said the seneschal. "I am your lord and master. Sign this paper."

"My lord," replied Finette, "I do not know how to write."

"Do you think that I know?" rejoined the seneschal in a voice that shook the house. "Do you take me for a clerk? A cross is the signature of chevaliers." He made a huge cross on the paper, and handed the pen to Finette. "Sign," said he. "If you are afraid to make a cross, your arrest is declared, miserable girl, and I will see to its execution."

While speaking, he drew his heavy sword from its scabbard, and flung it on the table.

The only answer Finette made was to jump out of the window, and run to the stable to hide herself. The seneschal pursued her; but, when he tried to enter, an unexpected obstacle prevented him. The terrified cow had retreated at the sight of the young girl, and blocked up the doorway, while Finette seized the animal by the horns, and shielded herself behind her.

"You shall not escape me, sorceress," cried the seneschal; and, with an arm as strong as

Hercules, he seized the cow by the tail, and drew her out of the stable.

"*Abracadabra!*" exclaimed Finette. "May my cow's tail hold you, wicked man, and you hold my cow's tail, until you have been round the world together."

Instantly the cow started off like lightning, dragging after her the unhappy seneschal. Nothing stopped the two inseparable ones; they raced over mountains and valleys, traversed marshes,

rivers, and thickets; glided over the seas without drowning; froze in Siberia, melted in Africa; climbed the Himalaya Mountains and descended Mount Blanc, and at length, after an unparalleled journey of thirty-six hours, breathless and exhausted, arrived at

the great square of the village of Kerver.

A seneschal hanging on to a cow's tail is a sight not seen every day, so all the vassals and serfs assembled to admire the spectacle. But, mangled as he was by the cacti in Barbary, and the hedges in Tartary, the seneschal had not lost his majestic air. With a threatening gesture, he dispersed the vulgar crowd, and, limping sadly, returned to his house, there to take the refreshments and repose of which he began to feel the need.

VI.

WHILE the squire, the bailiff, and the seneschal were suffering these little annoyances, of which they did not care to boast, a great event was in preparation at the castle, nothing less than the marriage of Yvon and the fair-haired lady.

All the preparations were made, all the friends had come from within twenty leagues, and, one fine morning, Yvon and his bride, with the lord

and lady of Kerver, took their seats in a large
chariot adorned with green leaves, and journeyed
with great pomp toward the celebrated Monastery
of St. Maclou. On the right and left hand, an
hundred chevaliers, clad in armor and mounted
on gaily-dressed palfreys, accompanied the betrothed. As a mark of respect, each one had
his visor up, and his lance at rest. Near each
baron, a squire, also on horseback, bore the
lord's banner. At the head of the procession,

the seneschal pranced, a golden staff in his hand.

On the right and left hand, an hundred chevaliers, clad in armor
and mounted on gayly-dressed palfreys, accompanied the betrothed.

Behind the chariot walked the bailiff gravely, followed by the vassals and their wives; while the squire marshalled the serfs and retainers, an unruly and curious throng.

A league from the castle, on crossing a stream that divided the road, one of the swing-bars of the chariot broke. It was necessary to stop. The damage repaired, they whipped up the horses; but they pulled with such force that the new swing-bar broke into three pieces. Six times they renewed the piece of wood, six times it broke, without they being able to emerge from the rut in which the chariot was fastened.

Every one had something to say: the retainers, as well as wheelwrights and mechanics, were not behind-hand. That emboldened the squire: he approached the baron, doffed his cap, and, scratching his head, —

"My lord," said he, "in that house that shines among the trees, there lives a stranger who does nothing like any one else. Get her to lend you her tongs for a swing-bar. I think they will hold until to-morrow."

The baron nodded, and the retainers hastened to Finette's house. She obligingly lent them her golden tongs. They were put in the place of the bar, the bolts slipped, the horses cut, and away went the chariot as light as a feather. Every one was overjoyed; but their delight did not last long: an hundred paces on, the bottom of the carriage cracked and fell out. A little more, and the noble family might have disappeared entirely, as if they had fallen in a hole. Instantly wheelwrights and carpenters applied their skill; planks were sawn, nailed with heavy blows: in the twinkling of an eye the accident was repaired.

Forward, Kervers! Off they started; half the carriage remained behind; the Lady of Kerver remained sitting by the bride, while Yvon and the baron were borne off at a gallop. There was great despair over this fresh accident; all efforts

were vain : three times was the chariot mended,
and three times it broke. It seemed as if every
thing was bewitched.

Everybody offered advice, which emboldened
the bailiff. He approached the baron, and, bow-
ing low, —

"My lord," said he, "in that house that shines
among the trees there lives a stranger who does
nothing like any one else. Ask her to lend you
the leaf of her door to make a floor for the chariot. I think it will last until to-morrow.

The baron nodded, and twenty retainers ran
to Finette's house. She very obligingly lent
them a leaf of her golden door. They laid the
board on the bottom of the chariot : it fitted it
as if it had been measured for the purpose.

On they started again : the monastery was in
sight, and they thought their troubles over.

Vain hope! Suddenly the horses stopped, and
refused to draw. They added to the four already
in, six, eight, ten, twelve, twenty-four : all in

vain; the carriage did not stir. The more they
whipped the horses, the deeper the wheels went

into the earth. What was to be done? It would
never do to go on foot. To go on horseback,
and enter the church like common people, was
not the custom of the Kervers. They tried to
lift the carriage, pushed the wheels, shouted and
called; they talked a great deal, but did not ad-
vance an inch. The day was almost gone, and
the time for the marriage already passing.

Everybody offered advice, which emboldened
the seneschal. He approached the baron, dis-
mounted, and, lifting his velvet cap, —

"My lord," said he, "in that house that shines
among the trees there lives a stranger who does
nothing like any one else. Ask her to lend you
her cow to draw the chariot, and I think the
beast will pull until to-morrow.

The baron nodded, and thirty retainers ran to
Finette's house. She very obligingly lent them
her cow with the golden horns.

To go to the church drawn by a cow was not
exactly what the ambitious bride had expected;
but it was better than stopping half way without
being married. The cow was harnessed in front
of the four horses, and all waited to see what the
boasted animal would do. But, before the coach-
man had cracked his whip, off started the cow, as
if she were about to go round the world again.
Horses, carriage, baron, betrothed, were all borne
along by the furious animal. In vain the cheva-

liers spurred their horses to follow; in vain the
vassals and retainers ran as fast as they could,

taking the shortest cuts.   The chariot flew as if
on wings: no bird could have followed it.

When they reached the door of the monastery,
the bridal party, slightly shaken by their rapid
course, wished to alight.

Every thing was in readiness for the ceremony;
the bride and groom had been long expected.
But, instead of stopping, the cow redoubled her
speed.   Thirteen times she ran round the mon-

astery with the speed of a windmill; then, suddenly taking the road to the castle by the shortest cut and across fields, she ran so fast that
the Kervers were almost jolted to pieces before
being safely housed within the four walls of the
old chateau.

VII.

For that day, there was no more thought of marriage; but the tables were set and the collation ready, and the baron was too noble a lord to dismiss his brave Bretons before they had eaten and drunk, according to custom; that is to say, from the setting to the rising of the sun, and sometimes longer.

All were invited to seat themselves. There were ninety-six tables, arranged in the form of a horse-shoe, in eight rows. In front of all, on a large platform covered with velvet, with a dais in the middle, was a table larger than the others, laden with fruit and flowers, not to mention the roasted bucks, and peacocks which smoked under their feathers. That was where the bridal party were to sit, in full view of every one, that nothing might be wanting to the pleasures of the fête.

The meanest vassal would have had the right to salute the married pair, and empty his glass of hydromel to the honor and prosperity of the great and powerful house of Kerver.

The baron bade the hundred chevaliers be seated at his table, with their squires behind them to wait on them. At his right, he placed the fair-haired lady and Yvon; but he left the place on his left vacant, and, calling a page,—

"Run, child," said he, "to the stranger who was so kind to us this morning. It was not her fault that the success exceeded her good wishes. Tell her that the Baron of Kerver thanks her for her services, and invites her to the wedding of Lord Yvon."

On arriving at the golden house, where Finette was weeping for her dear lover, the page bent one knee, and, in the name of the baron, invited her to follow him to the chateau to honor the wedding of Lord Yvon.

"Salute your master from me," replied the

young girl proudly, "and tell him, if he is too noble to come to my house, I am too noble to go to his."

When the page told the baron the reply of the stranger, he struck the table such a blow with his fist, that he sent three dishes flying into the air.

"By the great sun!" he cried, "that is spoken like a lady; and, at the very beginning, I count

myself beaten. Let my mare Isabel be saddled, and my page and squires prepare to accompany me."

The baron, followed by his splendid train,

alighted at the door of the golden house. He
offered his excuses to Finette, took her hand,
held the stirrup for her, and made her mount
behind him, no more nor less than if she had
been the Duchess of Brittany herself. He spoke

no word to her on the
way, out of politeness;
and, when they reached
the castle, he conduct-
ed her, with head un-
covered, to the seat of
honor he had chosen
for her.

The baron's depar-
ture created a great
commotion; his return
a still greater. Every one asked who that lady
was that the proud baron treated with so much
respect. To judge by her dress, she was a stranger. Could it be the Duchess of Normandy, or
the Queen of France? They called the squire,

the bailiff, and the seneschal, to learn the truth from them. The squire trembled, the bailiff grew pale, the seneschal colored; but they all three remained as mute as fishes. The silence of these important personages increased the universal admiration.

All eyes were fixed upon Finette, while she felt beside herself with anguish, for Yvon had seen her without recognizing her; had merely cast upon her an indifferent glance, and resumed his tender conversation with the fair-haired lady, who smiled contemptuously.

Finette, heart-broken, drew from her purse the golden ball, her last hope. While conversing with the baron, who was charmed by her wit, she rolled the little ball round in her hand, and whispered:

" Ball of gold, oh, lend your aid
To rescue an unhappy maid !"

Instantly the ball .began to grow larger and

larger, until it became a goblet of embossed gold, the most beautiful glass that had ever adorned the table of baron or king. Finette filled it herself with hippocrass, fragrant with spices, and, calling the seneschal, who stood behind her much agitated, —

"Good seneschal," said she in her sweetest voice, "carry this goblet to Lord Yvon: I wish to drink to his happiness; he will not refuse to oblige me."

Yvon carelessly took the glass that the seneschal offered to him on a golden salver. He bowed to the stranger, drank the hippocrass, and placing the glass on the table before him, turned again to the fair-haired lady, who occupied his whole attention. The lady seemed uneasy and dismayed. He murmured some words in her ear, which restored her good humor; for her eyes sparkled, and she let her hand rest on his arm.

Finette hung her head, and began to weep. All was over.

"My children," cried the baron in a loud voice. "fill your glasses. Let us all drink to the worth and beauty of the noble stranger who honors us with her presence. To the Lady of the Golden House!"

Every one joined in the toast; but Yvon contented himself with raising the glass to his lips.

Suddenly he started, and remained speechless, his mouth open, and his eyes fixed, like a man in a vision. In the golden goblet, as if in a mirror, Yvon beheld his past life. The giant was pursuing him; Finette was escaping with him; together they embarked on the ship that saved them both; with her he landed on the coast of Brittany. He left her but for a moment; she wept at his departure. Where was she? By his side, of course; who but Finette should be by Yvon?

He bent towards the fair-haired lady, and uttered a cry as if he had trod on a serpent. Then. tottering as if he were drunk, he rose and looked about him with wild eyes. But when he saw Finette, he wrung his trembling hands, and, in a voice choked by tears, —

"Finette!" he cried, hurrying to the stranger, "Finette, will you forgive me?" And he fell upon his knees.

Finette was but too happy to forgive; and before the end of the day she was seated by Yvon; and one may guess all that they said, alternately weeping and smiling.

And what became of the fair-haired lady? I do not know. At Yvon's cry she disappeared. The chronicle declares that there issued from

the castle and over the walls a hideous old woman, whom the dogs chased and barked at; and
all the Kervers think that the fair-haired lady
was none other than the sorceress, the giant's
god-mother. At all events, the fête, though in-
terrupted a moment, was resumed again, more
merrily than before.

The next morning, early, all went to the chapel,
where, to his great delight, Yvon wedded Finette,
who feared no more misfortunes. After that,
every one eat, drank, and danced for thirty-six
hours, without stopping to rest. The squire's
arms were a little lame; the bailiff rubbed his
back occasionally; and the seneschal found his
legs quite tired; but all three had a weight on
their consciences that they tried to remove, so
they frisked about like young people until they
fell down from exhaustion, and were carried
away.

Finette revenged herself in no other way. Her
only desire was to render all happy around her

that belonged in any way to the noble house of
Kerver. Her memory endured a long time in
Brittany; and, in the ruins of the old chateau,
they will still show you the statue of the good
lady, who holds five little balls in her hand.